That Old Barn

Jennifer Hobbs Zahn

Abbott Press books may be ordered through booksellers or by contacting:

Abbott Press
1663 Liberty Drive
Bloomington, IN 47403
www.abbottpress.com
Phone: 1-866-697-5310

Because of the dynamic nature of the Internet, any web addresses or links contained in this book may have changed since publication and may no longer be valid. The views expressed in this work are solely those of the author and do not necessarily reflect the views of the publisher, and the publisher hereby disclaims any responsibility for them.

Any people depicted in stock imagery provided by Thinkstock are models, and such images are being used for illustrative purposes only.
Certain stock imagery © Thinkstock.

ISBN: 978-1-4582-1836-0 (sc)
ISBN: 978-1-4582-1838-4 (hc)
ISBN: 978-1-4582-1837-7 (e)

Library of Congress Control Number: 2014922506

Print information is avaialable on the last page.

Abbott Press rev. date: 12/1/2015

abbott press

For my grandson, Elijah

From the time he was two, Little Guy would say,
"Nana, what's that old barn doing today?"

Though they'd ride by fast, Nana's eyes could tell
That it might not be long before that old barn fell.

Brown wood all rotten, walls leaning to the side—
A rusty old tractor was still left inside.

Headlights all dusty and paint peeling thin,
It was hard for the tractor to stay warm in the wind.

Even though that old barn was not very pretty,
Little Guy never saw it with pity,

Though the boards and the hinges seemed ready to fly
With the next strong wind way up to the sky!

Not a soul seemed to know the barn was longing for help,
So, soon he began to pray for himself...

"If you give me the chance to be rescued, I'd never
lean in the wind...Why, I'd be a strong barn forever!"

The tractor, too, was longing to say,
"Won't someone take me out of here today?"

But to Little Guy they both were as cool as could be,
And he dreamed of a day when up close he could see.

To forget all his troubles, sometimes barn could be silly,
On dark winter nights, he'd hide very quickly.

The barn played this game hoping Little Guy wouldn't see
Through the darkness the spot just where he would be..

But Little Guy always squealed with delight,
When predictably he saw the barn come into sight.

Though Nana drove fast, Little Guy's keen eyes
Saw clear through the shadows where that old barn tried to hide.

Now one day in Spring Little Guy turned to stare.
He noticed that part of the tin roof wasn't there!

All at once he knew old barn was in trouble
And with the next strong wind, it might turn into rubble.

Wondering how he could help, and then with great care,
Little Guy remembered that he could say a prayer.

He prayed that soon the farmer would send
Someone to make that old barn new again.

As for the tractor, Little Guy thought to say,
"Once barn is brand new, the farmer will take you away...

He'll fix up your headlights and paint you bright red,
And before you know it, you'll be plowing instead!"

Can you believe it?...The very next day,
Stacks of paints and brushes were set right by the hay.

With boxes of nails, hammers and new wood to boot,
Little Guy's prayer was answered in one gigantic swoop!

Little Guy said, "Nana, there's so much to do!
Do you think the farmer will let us help, too?"

She said, "That's a great idea, so, yes, we can ask
If he will allow us to help with the task."

So if one day you travel down Route 143,
A red, shiny barn is what you will see.

And if that old barn could show you its smile,
Why, you'd notice that too, from a far-a-way mile!

You never can tell on a dusty old road,
When a shabby old tractor or barn you'll behold...

So, pull over and take time to dream for awhile,
Because bright red, shiny barns never go out of style!

ABOUT THE AUTHOR

Jennifer Hobbs Zahn is a retired elementary school teacher with over 30 years' experience working with young children. She has always enjoyed writing stories and songs. These days Jennifer spends lots of time with her husband, daughter and grandson. This is her first published book.

Printed in the United States
By Bookmasters